Rabbit and Turtle Go to School

story by Lucy Floyd
illustrated by Christopher Denise

HARCOURT BRACE & COMPANY

Orlando   Atlanta   Austin   Boston   San Francisco   Chicago   Dallas   New York
Toronto   London

"Let's race to school," said Rabbit.

3

"You ride the bus, and I'll run.
On your mark, get set, GO!"

4

Rabbit ran fast.
He went up the mountain.

Rabbit ran very fast.
He went down the mountain.

Rabbit ran very, very fast.
He went to the park.

Turtle's bus rode by the park
and then to school.

"Let's race tomorrow," said Turtle.
"I'll give you a head start."